Be Happy.......

Be Kind.......

Be Mindful.......

Be Loving.......

Be Calm.......

Be Brave.......

Be Positive.......

Be Courageous.......

Be Grateful.......

Be Curious......

Be in Control of Yourself......

Be Confident.......

Be Creative.......

Be Inspiring.......

Be Compassionate.......

Be Unique.......

BE YOU!

This Book Belongs To

Timmy

This Book is Dedicated to very special people in my life

The Love of My Life, My Childhood Sweetheart

WWC III

We have been thru everything together…Since I met you at my Girl Scout meeting in Kindergarten, to now raising a family together, and everything in between. There is no one else is this world I would want to explore this outrageous thing called Life with. I love you more than words could ever express. You are the Peanut Butter to my Jelly!

And to my children…

You are truly inspirations. Your smiles, your laughter, your innocence, and your sense of adventure make life worth living. I am so blessed to have you in my life.

Love Always,

Danielle Maria

aka Mom

Dear Parents and Educators,

This book is excellent for Parents to read with their children and for Educators to incorporate into their Lesson Plans with their students. This will support children in acquiring coping skills, learn how to express their feelings positively, and how to enrich their social skills. Getting children to be able to identify and express their feelings in a constructive way will help them cultivate the skills that are necessary to manage their own emotions.

Before Reading The Book: There are many ways you can get your child invested and motivated to explore and discover their feelings.

Ask your child/student…. How Are you feeling today? What happened to you today that made you feel that way? When you felt the emotions that you were feeling, how did you express them?

Explain to your child/student that it is ok to have different feelings each day, but we need to identify our feelings and express them in a calm, composed and respectful way.

While Reading The Book: Make connections to the reading by stopping throughout the text, on certain emotions and feelings, and allow your child or student to express what they believe that feeling means to them. What does it mean to them to be angry sad, excited, happy, or even proud? Have them make a facial expression that coordinates with the feeling they are discussing.

After Reading The Book: Have your child or student write down a feeling from

The book that they identified with. Ask your child to write about a time in their life that they felt this way. How did they react when they felt this way? What are some ways they feel they could have handled the situation differently? What are some ways they feel they handled the situation well? If you are working with a younger child, have them draw a picture about how they were feeling. Then have the child verbally explain the picture. Tell them to use their descriptive words to discuss how they acted in the situation, how they handled the situation well and how they could handle the situation better next time

How Are You Feeling Today, Timmy Taco?

Illustrated by
noman art

Written By
Danielle Maria

My Name is Timmy!

My friends call me Timmy Taco.

Can you guess what my most favorite food in the whole entire world is??????

You guessed it......TACO's!!!!!!

I could eat Taco's every single day.

In Fact, I think I'm going on a Taco Diet.

What's that you say?

It's where you eat Tacos...Everyday...Like 20 times a Day!

Wouldn't that be AMAZING?!?!

What's your favorite food?

How are you feeling today?

I feel all kinds of emotions all throughout the day.

Hey, I'm just a kid.... Its ok to have different feelings.

Right now, I feel GREAT!

I am so HAPPY because it's my favorite day of the week.

Today is Tuesday. Guess what happens on Tuesdays at my house?!?

Its TACO TUESDAY!

As long as I had a good day in school, did my work, listened to directions and followed the rules, my mom makes me my favorite dinner! I feel so HAPPY when she does this for me!

I was feeling so **PROUD** of my self today!

I got the **KINDNESS** award at school.

What an honor it was.

I read the Kindergarten class their favorite book.

My teacher said I did a great job.

She even let my principal know how well I did.

And then...I got a Kindness Certificate and Medal!

I couldn't believe it!

It feels great to help others. It really made me feel so PROUD!

What are some things you have done that made you feel **PROUD?**

I am so EXCITED!!!!!!

Today is my Birthday! I am having a big birthday party. My mom said that I have been so good, that she let me invite my entire class! They are all coming to celebrate with me.

I get to play with my friends, run around, bounce on the bouncy houses. And the best part of all, CAKE!!

I am so EXCITED that I couldn't even sleep last night!

It feels great to have so many people care about me, and I am so EXCITED to celebrate my special day with them!

It is great to have all of these fabulous feelings!

Sometimes I feel HAPPY, PROUD or EXCITED.

Those are all such positive ways to feel.

It makes me get all warm and fuzzy inside.

When I feel HAPPY, PROUD and EXCITED, I want others to feel the same way I do. So I do whatever I can to cheer someone up, be compassionate, and be a great friend.

We have to be MINDFUL of our actions.

And Always Choose KIND!

If you are having a great day, and your feeling **HAPPY**, **PROUD** or **EXCITED**, you should share that with someone else. Do something kind for someone, so that they can feel the same way that you are feeling.

I know what you're thinking…

Hey, I'm just a kid, how can I help someone feel special?!

Well, I'm glad you asked. There are so many ways to do something kind for someone, to make them feel **HAPPY**, **PROUD** or EXCITED.

Draw someone a picture or write them a letter.

Tell someone that you care about them or give a hug.

Visit someone that you haven't seen in a while.

Help clean up around your house, ESPECIALLY YOUR ROOM!

Read a book to your little brother, sister, or even a friend.

There are so many things that you can do to help others feel **HAPPY**, **PROUD**, and **EXCITED**!

What are you going to do to make someone **HAPPY** today?

Other days are not so great for me. This one day, I was feeling rather **SAD**. You see, my Grandma moved to Florida. That is so far from my house! You have to take a plane to get there.

I was looking at pictures, and I saw so many with my Grandma and me.

It made me feel so **SAD**, and I started to cry.

Then I realized that its ok to feel **SAD**. But what can I do to make this go away? I put my thinking cap on, and came up with a great idea......

I can call my Grandma on the video chat!

I can talk to her, and see her face, just as if she was here. I called her and we talked for hours! A few days later, I got a special delivery in the mail.

My grandma sent me a framed picture of our **Family**.

Now whenever I am feeling **SAD**, I can look at the picture, or call my Grandma on video chat and the sadness goes away.

Sometimes I feel so FRUSTRATED!!!!!!

I want to do my best but I'm struggling to figure out how!

Every time I try, I feel like I just keep failing.

I want to quit and give up, put my head under a blanket and

just close my eyes.

But then I realize.... What good will that do?

I want to be able to accomplish this. I want to do my best.

Even if I don't succeed, at least I can say I gave it a chance.

Mistakes are our way of showing at least we tried!

So instead of getting FRUSTRATED, instead of giving up....

I take a DEEP breath, I close my eyes,

and I tell myself I can try try try!

Other days are even worse, because sometimes I just get so
ANGRY!!!!

But let me explain to you why....

I have this little annoying brother who drives me CRAZY!!!!

When I came home from school today, he was in my room....
coloring on my walls and playing with MY toys.

I wanted to scream, I wanted to shout, I wanted to stomp my feet
and kick him right out!

Instead of expressing my ANGER, in an unhealthy way,

I decided to do a little twirl, jump up in the air, balance on one
foot, wiggle and giggle, take a deep breath...and CALM DOWN!

I realized that it wasn't that bad. That he wasn't being cruel.

He just wants to be like me, so he is ONE COOL DUDE!

Its ok to have different emotions, such as ANGRY, FRUSTRATED and SAD…

But its how we deal with our emotions, that can make the situation go from zero to BAD!

If you find yourself getting ANGRY, FRUSTRATED or even SAD,

Close your eyes, take a deep breath, and let's not get too MAD.

Remember that no matter what made you feel this way,

You can still go on to have a better day!

Be the better person, think about your self-control,

Think of ways to calm you down, maybe go for a quick stroll.

Some days are good,

Some days are bad.

The way you handle it,

Shouldn't make you **SAD**.

From **HAPPY** to **GLAD**,

To **ANGRY** or MAD...

We are allowed to have different feelings.

There are tons of feelings

That we feel each day.

Its ok to have these feelings,

We just have to express it the right way!

Timmy Taco has different feelings

All throughout the day...

But he has learned to portray his feelings,

In a healthy and positive way!

"*Reading Takes Your Mind On A Journey To Greatness!*"

Danielle Maria

Tips for working with children to express their feelings

Be a role model

Listen to your child

Talk with your child about different feelings

Reward positive behavior

Provide consistent consequences for negative behavior

Give your child choices

Work together to come up with solutions for managing negative behavior

Work on the child's self-control

Have your child draw a picture to express themselves

Recognize when your child is having a difficult moment...go for a walk, practice breathing techniques, or use calming strategies

Calming Corner

Have a Calming Corner for your child or student. This should be a quiet place where they can go to regroup for a short period of time. Provide books, coloring materials, a comfy place to sit, or even soft music.

Allow your child or student time to calm themselves down and then they can bring themselves back to the situation. The calming corner is not a punishment. It is a reward for the child or student to be able to use coping skills to calm themselves down and regulate their own emotions.

A special Thank You to my closest friends. You have been there thru thick and thin. Together we have gone from carefree girls to successful women raising beautiful families. While we may not see each other as often as we like, we can always pick up right where we left off. Thank you for being apart of my life, I would be lost without you!

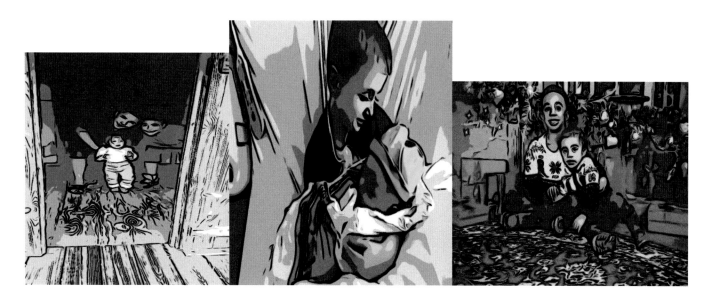

Be Happy.......

Be Kind.......

Be Mindful.......

Be Loving.......

Be Calm.......

Be Brave.......

Be Positive.......

Be Courageous.......

Be Grateful.......

Be Curious......

Be in Control of Yourself.......

Be Confident.......

Be Creative.......

Be Inspiring.......

Be Compassionate.......

Be Unique.......

BE YOU!

Made in the USA
Coppell, TX
04 January 2020